SUPERHERO SCHOOL

Curse of the Evil Custard

Alan MacDonald

Illustrated by Nigel Baines

BLOOMSBURY

LONDON NEW DELHI NEW YORK SYDNEY

Bloomsbury Publishing, London, New Delhi, New York and Sydney

First published in Great Britain in August 2015 by Bloomsbury Publishing Plc
50 Bedford Square, London WC1B 3DP

www.bloomsbury.com

Bloomsbury is a registered trademark of Bloomsbury Publishing Plc

A CIP catalogue record for this book is available from the British Library

ISBN 978 1 4088 2525 9

Printed and bound in Great Britain by CPI Group (UK) Ltd, Croydon CR0 4YY

1 3 5 7 9 10 8 6 4 2

MEET THE
SUPERHEROES
OF
MIGHTY HIGH...

DANGERBOY (aka Stan)

SPECIAL POWERS: Radar ears that sense danger

WEAPON OF CHOICE: Tiddlywinks

STRENGTHS: Survival against the odds

WEAKNESSES: Never stops worrying

SUPER RATING: 53

FRISBEE KID (aka Minnie)

SPECIAL POWERS: Deadly aim

WEAPON OF CHOICE: 'Frisbee anyone?'

STRENGTHS: Organised, bossy

WEAKNESSES: See above

SUPER RATING: 56

BRAINIAC (aka Miles)

SPECIAL POWERS: Super brainbox

WEAPON OF CHOICE: Quiz questions

STRENGTHS: Um . . .

WEAKNESSES: Hates to fight

SUPER RATING: 41.3

PUDDING THE WONDERDOG

SPECIAL POWERS: Sniffing out treats

WEAPON OF CHOICE: Licking and slobbering

STRENGTHS: Obedience

WEAKNESSES: World-class wimp

SUPER RATING: 2

MEET POTTY SCIENTIFIC GENIUS...
DR SINISTER
My greatest invention: EVIL CUSTARD!
yum

Chapter 1

Bad News

It was the first day of a new term. Stan, Miles, Minnie and Pudding the Wonderdog entered through the tall iron gates of Mighty High. During the long summer holidays little exciting

or dangerous had happened, so it was good to be back together as **the Invincibles**, probably the greatest superhero gang in Stan's class.

Stan looked around the playground, recognising the old familiar faces. Over the far side a group of boys were playing aerial football, occasionally sending the ball high into the clouds. Tank, the school bully, had found some new kids to play with and was amusing himself by throwing them over a wall.

All in all, it seemed like just another day at Mighty High … but that was about to change.

Miss Marbles, the head teacher, walked by wearing a worried expression and two pairs of spectacles on her head.

'Morning, miss,' said Minnie brightly.

Miss Marbles looked round, quickly stuffing a letter into her pocket.

'Morning? I suppose it is,' she said. 'How are you, Molly?'

'Minnie,' said Minnie. 'Is everything OK?'

'Yes, of course,' said Miss Marbles. 'Absolutely splendid, tip-top, couldn't be better. Well, I must be – you know, things to do.'

They watched her cross the playground and disappear through a door, coming out a second later when she realised it was the caretaker's shed.

Minnie frowned. 'You think she's all right?' she asked.

'Mad as a sack of cats,' said Miles.

'But she seemed a bit funny,' said Minnie. 'She's never called me Molly before.'

'She calls me "Stanley",' grumbled Stan.

'Well, that's your name,' said Miles.

'Yes, but how many superheroes do you know called Stanley?' asked Stan.

'You can be the first.' Miles grinned. '*Super Stanley*.'

'I'll stick to Dangerboy, thanks,' said Stan, who owed his nickname to his super-sensitive ears, which alerted him to danger.

Minnie was still thinking about Miss Marbles. 'Something's wrong,' she said. 'Maybe we ought to go and check on her.'

'Check on her?' said Stan. 'She's a head teacher, not a baby!'

'You go,' said Miles. 'I'm not getting into trouble.'

Pudding barked and wagged his tail.

'See? Pudding agrees with me,' said Minnie. 'Are you coming or not?'

Five minutes later they were knocking on the head teacher's door.

'Come in!' said Miss Marbles.

They found the head sitting at her desk with her marmalade cat asleep on her lap. There was an official-looking letter spread out in front of her.

'Ah, thank you for coming, have a seat,' she said, as if she'd been expecting them. 'I suppose your ears have been talking, Stanley?'

Stan looked baffled. His ears always tingled when trouble was in the air, but on this occasion they weren't even itching.

'Um, not really,' he said. 'Is there a problem?'

'You could say that,' replied Miss Marbles. 'I've had a letter this morning. It seems we're to have an inspection.'

Minnie stared. 'A police inspection?'

'If only,' laughed Miss Marbles. 'No, this is a school inspection. Every few years they send inspectors to look at the school to see if it's up to scratch, meeting national standards and so on.'

'Well, aren't we? I mean, meeting national wotsits?' asked Stan.

Miss Marbles leaned forward, clasping her

17

hands. The cat on her lap woke up with a jolt.

'Let me ask you something,' said the head. 'How much do your parents know about what we do here?'

Stan shrugged. 'Not much,' he said. 'They just think I go to a school for gifted children. If I told them the truth they'd never believe me.'

'Exactly.' Miss Marbles nodded. 'And that's the way I'd like to keep it. The fact is, our work at Mighty High is a carefully kept secret. No one knows we are teaching you to develop superpowers. If they did, there'd probably be an almighty row. All kinds of questions would be asked.'

'You mean like why don't we wear blazers?' suggested Miles.

'Unfortunately, it goes deeper than that,' said Miss Marbles. 'When the school inspectors arrive they'll expect to see a normal school timetable — you know reading, writing and, um … that other one …'

superhero school kid

Normal school kid

Blazer

'Maths?' said Miles.

'Precisely. The sort of subjects you find in any school,' said the head teacher.

Stan thought he began to see the problem. None of the subjects they learned at Mighty

High could remotely be described as 'normal'. Professor Bird taught flying while other lessons included mind control, unarmed combat and 'inside the criminal mind'.

'But surely they'll see how important it is,' argued Minnie. 'There aren't any other schools for children like us.'

'I agree with you, Milly,' said Miss Marbles. 'But I doubt if the inspectors will see it that way. If we fail this inspection we could be in trouble. It's possible they could even close the school.'

'Close it?' cried Stan. 'They can't do that!'

'I'm afraid they can,' sighed Miss Marbles. 'So I have thought it over and there's only one way we can pass this inspection. We have to convince the inspectors that we are a plain, ordinary school teaching normal children.'

Stan, Minnie and Miles looked at each

other. This was going to be a tall order. Mighty
High wasn't a large school, but every one of
the pupils possessed some weird or amazing
power – from changing colour to
hurricane-force burping.

'You mean we can't use our superpowers?'
asked Minnie.

'That's exactly what I mean,' said Miss Marbles.
'I want you all to behave as normally as possible.

Read your books, recite your times tables
and try not to set off any explosions. Can you
do that?'

'We can,' said Stan. 'But what about the
others?'

'I will talk to them in assembly,' said Miss
Marbles. 'The future of the school depends on this.'
She got up, dumping the cat on the floor,
and walked them to the door.

'One last thing,' she said. 'I'll need some volunteers to show the inspectors round the school. I thought you three could do it.'

'Seriously?' said Stan. 'Why choose us?'

Miss Marbles folded her arms. 'Well, your superpowers are ... how can I put it ... ?'

'Rubbish?' said Miles.

Knows Stuff

Sensitive Ears

Good with Frisbee

Super Eater

'Less obvious,' said Miss Marbles. 'Besides, I need sensible children.'

Stan raised his eyebrows. It was the first time anyone had ever accused him of being sensible.

DON'T BE GOOD, BE SUPER.

PROPERTY OF
MIGHTY HIGH SCHOOL

The Pocket Guide for Superheroes

Everything you need to know
to save the world.

2

SUPERPOWERS

THE TOP TEN

Whenever a bunch of superheroes get together — say at a bus stop or a costume party — sooner or later the talk will turn to the age-old question: which super power is the best?

Everyone has their own opinion, but here is my personal top ten.

1. FLYING

Flying is brilliant. Ask anyone, it's the power that's number one on their list. A word of warning though from personal experience — remember the golden rule.

Flying is an OUTDOOR ACTIVITY, not to be confused with Scrabble or Snakes and Ladders.

2. SUPER-STRENGTH

In any superhero gang there's always the muscle-bound hunk who shows off by lifting trucks or boulders above his head. I have just one word to say about this superpower: tickling!

3. SHAPESHIFTING

Wouldn't it be useful if, in the blink of an eye, you could turn into a wolf, a bat or even a complete idiot? Some of your friends may have mastered the last one.

4. SUPER-SPEED

If you can't fly, then running like the wind is the next best thing — especially when faced by an angry three-headed monster or a teacher (or worse, an angry three-headed teacher).

5. ELASTICITY

Legs of rubber, arms as bendy as a drinking straw — never challenge these guys to a game of basketball.

6. INVISIBILITY

Useful for those tricky moments when you've broken the TV/window/toaster.

7. TELEKINETIC POWERS

Use your mind power to make lifeless objects move. Warning: generally doesn't work on older brothers.

8. MAGNETISM

Amaze your friends when you make metal spoons, forks or coins stick to your body. Come to think of it, the usefulness of this one escapes me.

9. TIME TRAVEL

Ever made a bad mistake or messed up an exam? With time travel you can go back in time and mess up as many times as you want.

10. INVINCIBILITY

Probably the daddy of all superpowers, but this one should be handled with care. Many a superhero has claimed to be invincible, but not all of them lived to tell the tale.

Chapter 3
A Cold Welcome

The following week Stan and his friends stood by the main doors, waiting for the inspectors to arrive. They had ditched their capes and **Invincibles** costumes in favour of ordinary school uniforms. Unfortunately the only uniforms they owned belonged to their previous schools, which meant that they were dressed in three different colours.

Stan fiddled with his tie, uncomfortably. 'How are we going to recognise them?' he asked.

'They're inspectors – they probably look like teachers,' said Minnie.

'Most of our teachers look bonkers,' Miles pointed out.

This was true enough, but then most of the staff at Mighty High taught bonkers subjects. Stan looked up and down the road. He wished Miss Marbles had picked someone else to show the inspectors around. It was a big responsibility. What if they made a bad impression or one of them let something slip about the school? It was all very well for Miss Marbles to say they should act normally, but that meant *not* doing the things they normally did. Just thinking about it tied Stan's brain in knots.

'What do we say to them?' Stan worried.

'Relax. Just smile and be polite,' said Minnie. 'Once they arrive we can take them to see Miss Marbles.'

Stan nodded. He hoped Pudding didn't start sniffing round the inspectors' trousers. How did they explain what a dog was doing in school anyway?

Stan had suggested hiding him in a store cupboard but Minnie said that would be cruel. She claimed that Pudding was practically invisible to teachers anyway – they never seemed to notice him.

Just then, a dark blue car drove slowly past the gates.

'For goodness' sake, leave your ears alone,' sighed Minnie.

'I can't help it, they just started itching,' said Stan.

Meanwhile, around the corner, two shadowy figures had emerged from behind a lamp post.

They made a curious pair — one of them was a giant, while his companion could almost fit inside his pocket. The small man had a pointed beard, cold eyes and padded insoles in his shoes to make him look taller.

'This is the school,' said Dr Sinister.
'Mighty High.'

'Yesh, master,' said Otto, his large pea-brained bodyguard. He lifted his master up so that Dr Sinister could see over the railings.

'The question is, how do we get in?' asked Dr Sinister.

'Er … frough the door?' suggested Otto.

'It's a school, you idiot,' snapped Dr Sinister. 'You can't just walk in and say, "Please may we borrow one of your kiddiewinks to conduct an evil experiment?"'

'Yesh, master,' said Otto.

'And stop saying "Yesh master", you sound like a parrot!'

Dr Sinister rolled his eyes. Otto was loyal and strong as an ox but you might as well talk to a brick. Sometimes Dr Sinister longed for the company of other geniuses like himself. Since his disgrace at the *Scientist of the Year* awards, his fellow scientists had turned their backs on him – but not for long.

SCIENTIST OF THE YEAR AWARD

Once they were under the spell of Evil Custard, they would all become his willing slaves. Nobody would ever call him 'Dr Whatsitsname' again.

A dark blue car pulled up and a man and woman got out.

'Excuse me, is this school Mighty High?' asked the annoyingly tall woman.

Otto opened his mouth.

'Yes, it is,' said Dr Sinister. 'Can I help you?'

'No, just checking.' The woman smiled. 'I'm Miss Miller and this is Mr Long – we're school inspectors. Can't have us turning up at the wrong school, can we?'

Inspectors? Dr Sinister narrowed his eyes. But this was ideal, the perfect opportunity! The two inspectors would be expected at the school. They'd have complete freedom to nose around and speak to any of the children. If one or two kiddies happened to go missing, then who was going to notice? He reached up, offering his hand to the woman.

'Splendid, we've been expecting you,' said
Dr Sinister.

'You have?' said Miss Miller.

'Yes, I'm the head teacher, Mr ... Whackem.
I've been looking out for you.'

The inspector frowned and took out a letter from her briefcase.

'But I thought the head was ... a Miss Marbles?' she said.

'Ah, that's right, she is.' Dr Sinister thought quickly. 'But she was suddenly taken ill. Yesterday, in fact – with, erm ... zebrapox.'

'Zebrapox?' repeated Mr Long.

'Yes, it's like chickenpox only you come out in stripes,' said Dr Sinister.

'But never mind, I'm here to welcome you and this is our, er ... our school secretary, Mr Otto.'

The inspectors stared at the man mountain, who smiled back, revealing a mouthful of gold teeth. He looked more like an Olympic weightlifter than a school secretary.

Miss Miller frowned. 'I don't know, this is all very odd,' she said.

Dr Sinister's eyes opened wide and he suddenly changed his voice. 'Follow me,' he said.

'What?'

'Do exactly what I say. Follow me.'

The inspectors nodded, falling under the spell of his staring eyes and hypnotic voice.

Dr Sinister took them round to the back of the school, where they climbed in through a gap in the fence. Hurrying across the playground, he opened a couple of doors, one of which turned out to be a shed. Finally he found a way into the school and clicked his fingers. The inspectors came out of their trance. Dr Sinister descended some stairs into a damp, dimly lit basement, where a smell of boiled cabbage and potato hit them immediately.

'Are you sure this is right?' asked Miss Miller, uncertain how she'd got there.

'Where are the children?' asked Mr Long.

'Oh, they're about somewhere,' replied Dr Sinister. 'First we'll stop by at my office. By the way, may I see your badges?'

SCHOOL INSPECTOR
MR LONG
OFFICIAL USE ONLY

Both inspectors handed them over and Dr
Sinister quickly pocketed them. He opened a
metal door and stood aside for them to go in.

'Please, make yourselves comfortable,' he
insisted.

Miss Miller peered into the head's office.
'It's pitch dark,' she objected.

'And freezing cold,' said Mr Long, going in.
'Are you sure this … ?'

44

'Fools!' laughed Dr Sinister as he turned the key, locking them in. 'A few hours in the freezer will cool them down. Heh heh heh!'

'HA! HA! HA!' chortled Otto. 'Who was they again?'

'School inspectors, dummy,' answered Dr Sinister. 'But you and I are going to take their places. Here's your badge, Otto. Pin it on your jacket. You can be Miss Miller.'

'Fank you, master,' said Otto, who'd never had a badge before.

'Now, we are going to take a look around the school,' said Dr Sinister. 'While we're here, try not to talk, and I don't want you eating anything.'

Otto's face fell. 'Not even a lickle caterpillar?'

'Especially not a lickle caterpillar,' said Dr Sinister. 'And remember, we are school inspectors, so don't call me master.'

Otto nodded gravely. 'Yesh, master.'

Chapter 4
Weird Science

Stan checked his watch. Something was wrong – the inspectors should have arrived half an hour ago.

'Maybe they're not coming,' he said hopefully.

'You don't think we could have missed them?' asked Minnie.

'I don't see how, but someone ought to tell Miss Marbles,' said Stan.

His ears were still bothering him.

Sometimes they itched and prickled for no reason at all. Looking around, Stan almost jumped out of his skin. Behind him stood two strange men who had appeared from nowhere. One was tiny and bearded, while his companion was as big as a wardrobe and very interested in a fly on the wall.

'Leave it,' ordered the little man. 'Good morning, we are the school inspectors. I'm Mr Long and this is er ... Miss Miller.'

'Right,' said Stan.

He knew he was staring, but he'd never met inspectors before and these two looked like they'd escaped from a circus. For a woman, Miss Miller was remarkably big and hairy. Equally odd was how they'd managed to get into school without anyone seeing them.

Minnie broke the silence. 'I'm Minnie. Welcome to Mighty High,' she said, stepping forward. 'This is Stan and Miles, and that's Pudding, the one with the tail.'

TAIL

Pudding growled
and crouched
low, baring
his teeth.

Miss Miller growled back, which sent
Pudding running to hide behind Minnie's legs.

'It's OK, Puds, they won't hurt you,' said
Minnie. She turned to the inspectors. 'Miss
Marbles is in her office; she's expecting you,'
she said.

They led the way down the long corridor
and Minnie knocked on the head teacher's
door. Miss Marbles was wearing her best
dress for the occasion, along with most of her
jewellery. It looked like she was planning to
charm the inspectors – either that or take them
ballroom dancing.

'Come in, come in. Welcome!' she gushed, shaking hands with her visitors. 'May I offer you some refreshment? Tea? Coffee? Milk? Hot chocolate? Sherry? Cakes? Biscuits?'

'No, thanks,' said Dr Sinister. 'We're not hungry.'

'I am,' said Otto. 'Have you any lickle ...'

'Shut up,' snapped his master. He gave them a thin smile. 'If you don't mind, we've a lot of inspecting to get through, you know – children, books, pencils and so on.'

'Pencils?' said Miss Marbles.

'Yes. Sharp pencils, sharp minds,' said Dr Sinister. 'Shall we make a start?'

'Of course,' said Miss Marbles. 'But I'm afraid you'll find us very dull. Just a plain, ordinary school like any other, isn't that right, Stanley?'

'Oh, erm, yes,' agreed Stan.

He caught Minnie's eye, wondering how many more whopping lies Miss Marbles planned to tell that day.

'The children can take you on a little tour,'
she said. 'Ask them any questions you like.'

'Just don't expect us to answer them,' Miles
muttered under his breath.

They set off. Miss Marbles had told them to
keep the tour of the school as brief and boring
as possible. She had warned all the staff to make

sure they taught 'normal' subjects today, such as English, science, maths or history. Any use of superpowers was strictly forbidden. All the same, Stan felt nervous as they walked to the hall. Not all the teachers were what you'd call reliable. Professor Bird was barking mad, while Professor Quirk usually nodded off in assembly and missed anything that was said. Stan thought it would be a miracle if they could get through the tour without any disasters.

Half an hour later they found themselves back at the empty hall.

'And this is the hall,' said Minnie. 'We use it for ...'

'Yes, we've seen it,' snapped Dr Sinister impatiently. 'What we haven't seen is any children. Let's take a look in here, shall we?'

Before they could stop him, the inspector opened a classroom door and barged into the middle of a lesson. Stan groaned. As luck would have it the teacher was Professor Quirk. It wasn't immediately obvious what he was teaching, but it didn't look like geography. A large wooden trunk stood on end at the front of class, bound by thick chains and padlocks. Professor Quirk glared at them.

'Do you mind?' he grumbled. 'I'm trying to teach a lesson here.'

'Please carry on,' said the small inspector, waving a hand. 'We are simply here to observe.'

Stan tried to catch Professor Quirk's eye.

'These are the *inspectors*, professor,' he said meaningfully.

'The WHAT?' barked the professor.

'The inspectors,' repeated Minnie. 'They wanted to see your *geography* lesson.'

'Geography? What are you talking about?' replied Professor Quirk, checking the stopwatch in his hand. 'One minute!' he bellowed.

A thump came from inside the trunk, making it rock. It dawned on Stan that there was someone inside and they were trying to get out!

Professor Quirk taught escapology – the art of escaping when you were bound, gagged or, in this case, padlocked in a box. He obviously hadn't got the message that he was supposed to be teaching something that belonged on a normal timetable.

Mr Long, the little inspector, approached the trunk.

'And what have we here?' he asked.

'Nothing,' said Stan quickly. 'Maybe we should get on; we haven't seen the, er … toilets yet.' He held the door open.

Deafening noises came
from the trunk, which finally toppled over with
an almighty crash.

'One minute, thirty-two!' shouted the
professor. 'Time's running out.'

The inspector looked
startled. 'There's someone in
there!' he said, pointing to
the trunk in astonishment.

'Er … possibly,' said Stan.

'Of course there's someone in there,' said Professor Quirk.

'But why would you lock someone inside a trunk?' asked the inspector.

'To see if they can escape, why do you think?' barked the professor.

Suddenly a large fist shot out of one side of the trunk, followed by a boot smashing a hole in the top. The inspectors stood back as more blows, thumps and crashes smashed the lid of the trunk open. Tank's head and shoulders rose from the broken shell like a magician's assistant, only uglier. He shook sawdust and splinters from his hair and let out a roar of triumph.

'Two minutes, ten seconds,' the professor announced, stopping his watch. 'Well done, Tank. Not pretty but certainly effective.'

Tank stepped out of what was left of the trunk and stomped back to his desk, rubbing his head.

The inspector folded his arms. 'So tell me, I'm curious, what lesson is this?' he asked.

Stan's mind had gone blank. He turned to Minnie hopefully but she shook her head.

'Science,' Miles blurted out, coming to the rescue.

'Science?'

'Yes, we've been testing the resistance of different materials – you know like iron, steel or copper,' explained Miles. 'In this case we were testing the resistance of wood against a heavy object, such as Tank's head.'

'Oh, I see,' said the inspector, clearly not seeing at all. 'Well good, good, please carry on.'

He looked around for his hairy colleague, who had found a spider's web hanging in a corner.

'Miss Miller, we are going!' he said, sharply.

Miss Miller stood up with a guilty expression. She seemed to have something in her mouth, which she swallowed quickly.

'Right,' said Professor Quirk. 'Tomorrow we'll be looking at escaping underwater. Read chapter seventeen in your textbooks ...'

Stan hurried the vistors out of the door before it got any worse. The lesson probably wasn't what Miss Marbles had in mind when she claimed they were a dull, ordinary school. The inspectors, however, seemed to have other things on their minds.

'Do you have school dinners?' asked Mr Long.

'Not if we can help it,' said Miles.

Minnie nudged him to shut up. 'Mrs Sponge is in charge of dinners,' she explained. 'Her meals are always ... interesting.'

'That's one word for it,' muttered Miles.

'We can take you to the kitchens if you like,' offered Stan.

'That's all right, they're downstairs, aren't they?' said the inspector.

'Yes, we'll show you,' said Minnie.

'No, no, we know the way,' said the inspector. 'Thank you for the tour, it's been most interesting, but we can't keep you from your lessons. This way, Miss Miller.'

Stan watched the two of them head down the stairs. He slumped back against a wall. 'That was a disaster!' he groaned. 'Do you think they noticed?'

'What, Tank escaping from a trunk by smashing it to bits?' said Miles. 'Pretty hard to miss, I'd say.'

'But they didn't seem that bothered,' said Minnie thoughtfully.

'In any case, we shouldn't have let them go off on their own,' said Stan. 'Miss Marbles said to stay with them.'

'There's something else I don't understand,' said Minnie. 'Did you notice them checking our work or looking at our books?'

'No,' answered Stan.

'Exactly,' said Minnie. 'Wouldn't inspectors

take notes and write stuff down?'

Miles grinned. 'I'm not sure the big one knows *how* to write,' he said.

'That's the other weird thing,' said Minnie. 'I keep thinking I've seen the small one before somewhere. And the big one, Miss Miller, I'm sure she's a man. Also, I was watching her back there and she ate a spider!'

'She WHAT?' said Stan.

'I'm telling you, she put a big hairy spider in her mouth and swallowed it.'

Miles shook his head. 'Maybe they won't think our school dinners so bad after all,' he said.

Chapter 5

A Spoonful of Evil

Down in the damp, dingy kitchens, Mrs Sponge, the world's worst cook, was preparing lunch for that day. She stirred a saucepan of thick lumpy custard as it bubbled on the stove.

CLUNK!

She frowned. What was that noise? She'd heard it more than once that morning – a sound like something knocking or mice learning to tap dance.

She put her ear close to the saucepan and listened. No, it wasn't the custard. She wandered out into the corridor and waited for a moment.

THUMP! THUMP!

There it was again! The noise almost
sounded as if it was coming from the freezer
room. She crept slowly down the corridor and
reached out a hand to the door.

'Ah, there you are!'

The voice made her jump. She turned to see
two strange men standing at the foot of the stairs.

'Mrs Sponge, isn't it?' said the little
bearded man. 'We are the school inspectors,
Mr Long and Miss Miller.'

Miss Miller grinned and cracked her giant
knuckles. She didn't look like a 'miss', but
maybe she'd forgotten to shave that morning.

'Inspectors?' said Mrs Sponge, wiping her
hands on her apron. She wondered if she should

bow or curtsy. No one had told her anything about an inspection. If she'd known she would have polished the cutlery or at least got rid of the mouse droppings.

She pointed to the big freezer door.

'I know it's ridiculous but I thought I heard knocking,' she explained.

'Oh, I shouldn't worry,' laughed the inspector. 'It's probably your knees; it's very chilly down here. Now, we wanted to see the kitchens.'

Mrs Sponge led them inside.

Dr Sinister looked around. The place was a health hazard. Tins of soup lay open on the worktop, green fungus grew on the ceiling and the cooker had more stains than a butcher's apron.

'How many staff do you have?' he asked.

'Well, counting me … one,' replied Mrs Sponge.

'You're here by yourself?' said Dr Sinister.

This was child's play, he thought. There was no one around to interfere.

He peered at some thick yellow gloop bubbling in a pan. 'And what's this?' he asked.

'Custard,' replied Mrs Sponge. 'I'm serving it with apple pie. Would you like a piece?'

Dr Sinister accepted a small slice and spat it out instantly.

'EUGH! What's in it?' he said.

'Potatoes, mostly,' said Mrs Sponge.

'What? I thought you said it was *apple* pie?'

'Yes, but we ran out of apples,' explained the cook.

Dr Sinister shook his head. Quite possibly the old crone was mad. Certainly you'd have to be mad to eat her food. But then innocent schoolkiddies had little choice, which suited his purposes perfectly.

He drew a small glass bottle from the pocket of his coat. The green liquid caught the light as he held it up. 'You see this?' he said.

'Cough medicine?' asked Mrs Sponge.

'No, this is my secret ingredient for perfect custard,' said Dr Sinister mysteriously. 'A few drops of this and your custard will be transformed.'

'Ooh,' said Mrs Sponge. 'Does it get rid of lumps?'

'Believe me,' said Dr Sinister, 'anyone who tastes this custard won't even notice the lumps. You should try it. REALLY, I *WANT YOU* TO TRY IT.'

Mrs Sponge found herself transfixed by Dr Sinister's eyes and hypnotic voice.

'Try it?' she repeated.

'Yes,' said Dr Sinister. 'Take this bottle and pour a few drops into the custard. Do it now.'

The cook
obeyed. Three or
four drops of the
secret ingredient
spilled into the
saucepan. Immediately
the yellow gloop began
to froth and bubble
like a boiling sea.

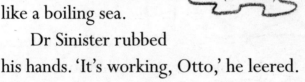

Dr Sinister rubbed
his hands. 'It's working, Otto,' he leered.

'Yesh, master,' said Otto. 'Can I lick the
spoon?'

'Don't be an idiot,' snapped Dr Sinister.
'It's not for the likes of you. No, we must take
this one step at a time. First we will try it
on the innocent sprogs and watch the effect.
Once it's perfected I will have my revenge on
all those fools who doubted my genius. Evil
Custard will make them my loyal creatures and I
their lord and master. HOO HA HA HAAAA!'

'What about her, master?' said Otto, pointing to Mrs Sponge, who seemed to have fallen into some kind of trance. Dr Sinister snapped his fingers and the cook blinked.

'I'm sorry, what were you saying?' She frowned.

'The custard,' said Dr Sinister. 'Try it, just take a lick.'

'Shall I?' said Mrs Sponge. She lifted the spoon to her lips and licked it. 'Mmm,' she said. 'That really does taste quite ...'

Mrs Sponge collapsed, falling to her knees and choking and spluttering.

'She's gone yellow,' said Otto. 'Is she dead?'

'Of course she isn't dead,' replied Dr Sinister. 'She only licked the spoon. But imagine what the effect will be if someone drinks a whole bowlful.'

'Who's gonna do that, master?' asked Otto.

Dr Sinister glanced at the clock on the wall and smiled. 'Oh look, it's gone twelve,' he said. 'Almost time for the little kiddies to have their lunch.'

Chapter 6
Second Helpings

Back upstairs, Stan and his friends ran into Miss
Marbles on their way to lunch.

'Ah, there you are, Stan,'
she said breathlessly. 'Now,
where are the inspectors?'

'They went downstairs to
see the kitchens,' replied Stan.

'What? You let them go on
their own?' Miss Marbles ran a
hand through her hair. 'That's the

last place we want them poking around,' she sighed. 'You know what Mrs Sponge's cooking is like – they might die of food poisoning!'

She was about to hurry off but Minnie spoke up. 'Miss Marbles,' she said. 'I keep thinking I've seen one of the inspectors before.'

'It's hardly likely,' replied Miss Marbles.

'I know, but there's something odd about them,' Minnie persisted. 'They don't *look* like inspectors. They don't even take notes or write anything down.'

'Minnie thinks they might be imposters or something,' laughed Stan.

Miss Marbles gave her a weary look. 'Really, Minnie, you've been reading far too many comic books,' she said. 'Of course they are inspectors, they're wearing *badges* for heaven's sake!'

She hurried off to find out where their visitors had disappeared to. Minnie folded her arms and glared at the boys. 'Well, thanks a bunch for backing me up,' she said.

'I did!' protested Stan.

'So did I!' said Miles. 'Maybe not out loud but I was thinking it!'

In the hall they joined the dinner queue where Mrs Sponge was serving lunch. A menu was scrawled in chalk on the blackboard. It read:

TODAYS MENU
―――――――――
delishus vegitable
Hotpot
desert: Appel Pie
and CUSTARD

Mrs Sponge's description of the meals she served was more hopeful than accurate. As a rule she just boiled whatever she had in the cupboard and then gave it a name.

'Apple pie and custard?' said Miles. 'That actually sounds OK.'

'I wouldn't get your hopes up,' warned Stan. 'Remember the trifle surprise last week!'

They shuffled forward until they reached the front of the queue. Mrs Sponge splodged watery brown hotpot on to their plates. Stan didn't think she was looking her normal self today – and the apple pie and custard looked even worse. They found an empty table and sat down. Stan rubbed his ear; it was giving him trouble again.

'Did you see Mrs Sponge?' he asked. 'She looks kind of yellow.'

'That's more than you can say for this custard,' said Miles. 'I think it's alive!'

The custard had a wobbly, jelly-like texture and gave off a faint luminous glow. Stan pushed his bowl away with a sigh, deciding it was safer to stick with the vegetable hotpot.

Just then Tank arrived and slumped into the seat next to him. Stan was surprised – it wasn't as if they were friends. Tank didn't really have any friends and he wasn't a big talker – generally he was too busy cleaning his plate and anyone else's he could get his hands on. Stan watched him swiftly work his way through the hotpot, slurping from his spoon. He was about to start on his dessert when he noticed Stan's full bowl.

'You eating that?' he demanded.

Stan shook his head. 'Not really.'

'Shame to waste it,' said Tank. 'Give it here.'

He piled the apple pie and glowing custard into his own bowl and attacked it, shovelling spoonfuls into his mouth. The others watched in disbelief.

'Not bad,' grunted Tank, wiping custard from his chin. 'Tastes a bit ...'

He broke off and let out a belch like a thunderclap.

His face turned white as his hand flew to cover his mouth.

The next moment he shot to his feet, knocking over his bowl, and bolted from the dining room.

Stan stared in surprise. 'What's got into him?' he asked.

'Probably too much apple pie,' said Miles.

But Minnie was looking at the bowl Tank had knocked over. Thick blobs of bright yellow custard had spilled out on to the table. They glowed and shimmered like radioactive matter.

Minnie bent to sniff them. 'I know the custard's always bad but this looks weird!' she said.

Stan was glad he'd given it a miss, and looking round the hall, he wasn't the only one. People had either left it on one side or were still eating their main course. Tank seemed to be the only one who'd eaten his dessert.

'Maybe I ought to check on him,' said Stan.

He hurried to the boys' toilets and knocked on the door.

'TANK? You OK?' he called.

There was no answer. Stan wondered whether he ought to go in but he didn't want Tank throwing up over his school shoes. He'd only cleaned them this morning. He tried again.

'Tank? Are you in there?'

Strange grunts and growls came from the toilets. If Tank was being sick, he was really making a meal of it.

Miles and Minnie appeared from the dining hall.

'Miss Marbles is coming,' said Minnie. 'Is he OK?'

'OOORRRROOW!' howled Tank.

'Probably not, then,' said Minnie.

'He'll be fine,' said Miles. 'Serves him right for being such a greedy pig.'

Stan wasn't convinced. 'I don't know,' he said. 'Maybe he ate something bad.'

'Like school dinners?' said Miles.

'Anyway, it's no good standing here. You'd better take a look,' said Minnie.

'ME? Why me?' protested Stan. 'We're not exactly best mates.'

'Well *I* can't go in, it's the boys' toilets!' said Minnie.

Stan stood rubbing his ear, which was tingling violently. (Never a good sign.) Luckily, at that moment, Miss Marbles arrived. 'I've looked in the kitchens; there's no sign of them,' she said crossly.

'Who?' asked Minnie.

'The inspectors, of course, and why are
you all standing outside the toilets?'

Stan briefly explained the situation and that
Tank was inside.

'Then we'd better check if he's all right,'
said Miss Marbles.

'Tank? It's me, Miss Marbles,' she called.
'I'm coming in.'

In reply there was a loud crash that made
the door shake. Miss Marbles had heard enough;
she swept in with the others behind her.

The room was empty.
One of the three
cubicle doors hung
off its hinges, while
the other two were
shut. Stan looked
at the others. He
had a really bad
feeling about this –
his ears were on fire.

'Tank? Are you OK?' said Miss Marbles.

No answer.

Miles edged towards the exit. 'Maybe we should come back later,' he suggested.

Suddenly something burst out of the last cubicle. It was Tank, or at least it had Tank's face. The rest of him had changed into a giant Blob Thing almost three times their size. His yellow skin dripped and wobbled as if it were made out of … out of

Chapter 7
Yellow Peril

Miss Marbles lay face down on the wet floor and let out a moan.

'Are you OK, miss?' asked Minnie, helping her to sit up.

'Apart from a few broken bones, fine,' groaned the head teacher.

Stan looked around the room. Broken glass littered the floor and there was a gaping hole in the wall where Tank had crashed through. Thick blobs of foul-smelling custard dripped down the walls. Miles reached out a finger.

'I wouldn't touch it!' warned Stan. 'We don't know if it's safe.'

'Are you sure that was Tank?' asked Miss Marbles. 'He looked … well, not himself.'

Stan had been thinking the same thing. Tank had seemed fine until he started on his dessert, which no one else had eaten.

'It must be the custard,' said Stan. 'There's something funny about it.'

'Well, it's always been lumpy,' admitted Miss Marbles.

'It's not just that,' said Stan, pointing to the splattered walls. 'It smells weird and gives off a kind of glow. Whatever's in it turned Tank into some kind of Incredible Blob Thing.'

Miss Marbles got gingerly to her feet. 'Well, there's nothing for it,' she sighed. 'There's the safety of the other children to consider. I will have to inform the inspectors.'

'Where are they, anyway?' asked Minnie.

'Good question,' said Miss Marbles. 'Just as this happens, they vanish into thin air.'

She went off in search of the visitors. Minnie stared at the dripping walls.

'I still don't trust those two,' she said. 'Did you notice Pudding was scared of them?'

'He's scared of everything,' said Stan. 'And anyway, the inspectors weren't here.'

'No,' replied Minnie. 'They were in the kitchens, which funnily enough is where the custard came from.'

Stan's eyes widened. Minnie had a point.
If there was something in the custard, then
someone must have put it there. It wasn't likely
to be Mrs Sponge, who was a terrible cook but
harmless. He headed out of the door.

'Now where are we going?' asked Miles,
catching up.

'To the kitchens, of course,' replied Stan.
'We've got to find out what's going on.'

They hurried down to the kitchens. On
top of the cooker, they found a saucepan
sticky with custard, which had dripped down

the sides. Stan wrinkled his nose. It gave off
the same nasty smell as the stuff on the toilet
walls. There was no sign of the two inspectors.
Pudding padded around
the kitchen, sniffing in
corners, then trotted
out. A moment later
they heard him barking
in the corridor.

'What's up with him?'
asked Miles.

'I think he's found something,' said Minnie.

Pudding began scratching at a metal door.

'What's kept in here?' asked Minnie. 'I've
never seen it before.'

'Me neither. Better take a look,' said Stan.

The door was heavy and padlocked. Once
they turned the key, it took two of them to
wrench it open. Inside was a giant freezer. It was
stocked with chickens, frozen vegetables and
two inspectors who'd turned blue in the face.

Chapter 8
World's Most Wanted

Five minutes later the two inspectors were
sitting by the warm radiator, wrapped in
blankets. Their teeth chattered so violently
they could hardly speak.

'You're the inspectors?' said Stan. 'Are you
sure?'

'Y … y … yes,' stammered Miss Miller.
'S … s … someone locked us in …'

'Did you see who it was?' asked Minnie.
Miss Miller nodded. 'The h … h …'

'Head dinner lady?' said Minnie.

'Headless ghost?' said Miles. Stan kicked him.

'N … no, the h … h … head teacher,' Miss Miller replied.

Stan looked surprised. Why on earth would Miss Marbles lock the school inspectors in the basement freezer? It didn't seem like the best way to make a good impression.

'This head teacher, what did she look like?' asked Minnie.

Mr Long shook his head. 'N … n … not she,' he chattered.

'He?' said Minnie. 'A little man with a beard?'

The inspectors both nodded at once.

'I knew it!' said Minnie, jumping up. 'It wasn't Miss Marbles, it was that strange little man we showed round the school.'

Miles was looking confused. 'I'm sorry,' he said. 'If these are the real inspectors, then who exactly are the other two?'

Minnie grabbed a copy of their textbook, *The Pocket Guide for Superheroes*, from among the cookbooks on the kitchen shelf. She flicked through until she came to the page she was looking for.

'I knew I'd seen him somewhere before!' she cried.

THE WORLD'S MOST WANTED

NUMBER 13: DR SINISTER

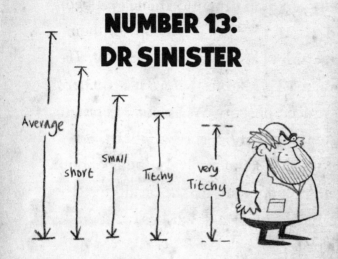

Description: Bald, bearded, but don't mention his height.

Career: Pint-pot evil genius, disqualified from *Scientist of the Year* awards when it turned out he'd voted for himself — one thousand times.

Evil Rating: 91

'See? That's him, Dr Sinister!' cried Minnie. 'He's here in our school, posing as an inspector. I told you!'

'Well, you didn't mention his name,' Miles objected.

'Never mind his name,' said Stan. 'We've got to warn Miss Marbles before it's too late!'

They raced upstairs. Whatever evil scheme Dr Sinister had in mind, it certainly wasn't improving school dinners. They dashed along the corridor and burst into the head's office, where Miss Marbles sat at her desk. She looked up in surprise.

'The inspectors!' panted Stan, out of breath.

Miss Marbles held up her hands. 'Calm down, I found them; everything's under control,' she said. 'I had a very nice chat with Mr Long. He advised me that the safest course of action was to close the school and send the children home. In fact, they should be getting on the bus now.'

'What bus?' said Minnie.

'Well, the school bus, of course. What other bus is there?'

Minnie ran over to the window. Outside the gates sat an old black bus, which looked like it had been rescued from a scrapyard. Children were beginning to climb on board.

'That's not our school bus!' said Minnie.

'And they're not school inspectors either,' said Stan. 'We've just found the real ones downstairs, locked in a freezer. The man you've been talking to is called Dr Sinister.'

'DR SINISTER!!!' said the head teacher. 'Who called a doctor?'

'He's not a *real* doctor, he's on the World's Most Wanted List!' said Minnie. She showed Miss Marbles the picture they'd found. The head teacher turned pale. She hurried to the window. 'QUICK!' she cried. 'Don't let them get on the bus!'

They raced outside, with Pudding joining the chase. But just as they arrived, the bus doors swung shut with a hiss. The vehicle pulled away with Otto at the wheel and their classmates on board. Dr Sinister's face appeared at the window and he gave them a cheery wave.

Miss Marbles clutched her head. She'd just allowed a wanted criminal to waltz out of the door, stealing practically every child in the school. It wasn't going to look too good on their report.

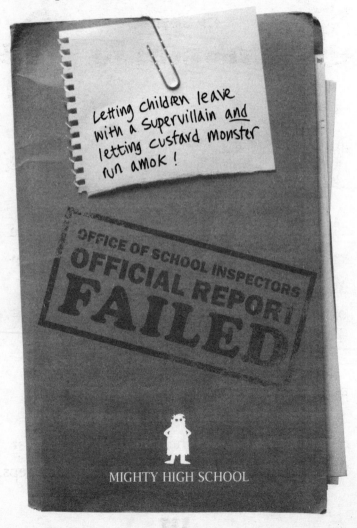

Chapter 9
The Evil Lair

They stood in silence as the bus sped away and vanished out of sight. Looking round, Stan saw Miss Miller and Mr Long had joined them, wrapped in their blankets. They had witnessed the whole disaster.

'This is terrible. I'm going to phone the police,' said Miss Marbles.

'There isn't time,' said Stan. 'Let us go after them.'

'YOU?' Miss Miller marched down the steps.

'This is a police matter. It's far too dangerous for children.'

Minnie shot Miss Marbles a look. 'You might as well tell them,' she said.

The head teacher nodded wearily.

'I'm afraid I wasn't totally honest on the phone,' she admitted. 'Mighty High isn't quite like other schools. The children we teach are, how can I put it ... they're rather advanced.'

Mr Long looked puzzled. 'You mean they do advanced maths?'

'No, I mean they have superpowers,' replied Miss Marbles. 'Stan, for instance, has extrasensory ears – they warn him of danger.'

The two inspectors looked at Stan as if they expected his ears to burst into flames. But there wasn't time to explain further. This was a job for …

THE INVINCIBLES

'Our costumes are in the changing rooms, we'd better hurry,' said Stan.

'Wait, there's one more thing,' said Miles. 'I guess you all know the three ingredients of custard?'

Stan rolled his eyes. 'Not really, and we don't have time,' he said.

'Milk, sugar and custard powder,' Miles went on. 'That's all you need.'

'SO? What's your point?' said Minnie.

'My point is, what's the one thing you NEVER put in custard?' asked Miles.

THINGS NOT TO PUT IN CUSTARD

'WHAT?' cried Stan, losing patience.

'Water,' replied Miles. 'You don't add water to custard because it will make it thin and runny. And if you remember, water was the one thing that scared Tank away.'

Stan thought back. It was true Tank had reacted to water like a scalded cat.

Minnie stared. 'Are you saying we can defeat Evil Custard with WATER?'

'It's a possibility,' said Miles. 'Water could be a kind of antidote, or anti-custard. That's why we should take some with us.'

'Fine, we will,' said Stan. 'But what if your brilliant theory is wrong?'

'Well, in that case it won't work,' said Miles shrugging his shoulders.

Stan shook his head. Miles was one of his best friends but sometimes Stan thought his superpower was driving people up the wall. Right now, though, they had other things to worry about, such as how to track down their kidnapped friends. The bus was long gone but Minnie had found something in the *Pocket Guide*.

'It says here we need to look for a secret hideout,' she said.

'If it's a secret, how do we find it?' asked Stan.

'That's the whole point,' replied Minnie. 'We're not looking for a flat or a bungalow. It'll be somewhere dark and creepy-looking – basically somewhere only a madman would choose. That's where we'll find Dr Sinister.'

They set off with Pudding out in front

on the trail of the scent. If the book was right about secret hideouts it probably ruled out the public library.

After an hour of trawling the streets and stopping at lamp posts, they found themselves in a dirty backstreet with high brick walls on either side.

Stan shook his head. 'This is another dead end,' he sighed. 'We're wasting time.'

Pudding padded off to sniff round a group of dustbins. He looked back at Minnie and barked.

'He's found something,' said Minnie.

'Probably something to eat,' grumbled Miles.

Minnie climbed on to one of the dustbins so that she could see over the wall.

'I knew it,' she said. 'Take a look at this!'

Stan and Miles climbed up beside her. Over the wall they could see a run-down, deserted factory with broken windows and a sagging roof. The signs made it clear that visitors weren't welcome.

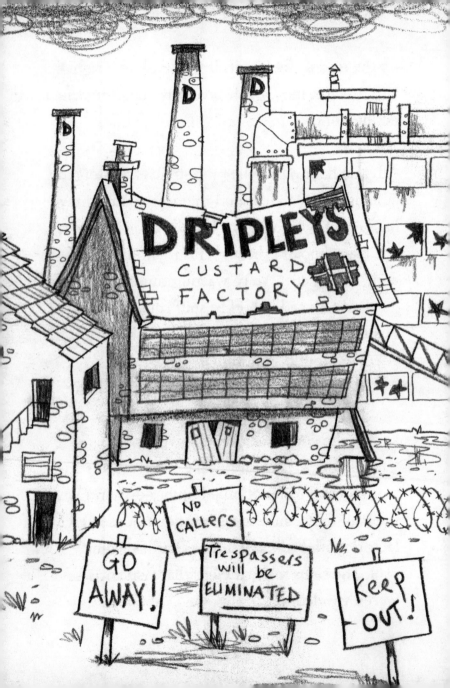

'A custard factory?' said Stan.

'It's perfect.' Minnie nodded. 'Just the place for making Evil Custard without attracting attention. And look over there.'

Parked in a backyard was a shabby black bus, the one that had driven off with their classmates on board.

Grey clouds gathered in the sky. The factory yard was deserted – but what lay inside? What did Dr Sinister want with a busload of children, and why bring them to a crumbling custard factory? Not for the first time, Stan's ears warned him they should go back – and not for the first time, he ignored them.

'Well?' said Minnie. 'What's the plan, then, Dangerboy?'

Stan hadn't the faintest clue. 'I guess we sneak in and try not to get caught,' he said.

'Hope for the best, you mean.' Minnie grinned. 'What's the worst that could happen?'

'We could end up like Tank,' said Miles

grimly. 'Everyone check your weapons.'

Stan checked his pockets and nodded. He hoped that Miles's theory about custard proved right – otherwise they'd all be coming to a sticky end.

Chapter 10
A Sticky End

The Invincibles crept into the shadowy custard factory. Pudding hung back at the door, because he was scared of the dark.

Stan's heart was beating fast. He wished criminals would leave the lights on so you could see where you were going. Once his eyes adjusted to the darkness he could make out tin drums and rusty machinery draped in cobwebs. The roof creaked in the wind.

'There's nobody here,' whispered Miles. 'Well, at least we tried.'

Stan shook his head and pointed to a doorway leading into the next room. They crept through, then halted in amazement. The room was like some sort of secret laboratory. At the top of a small flight of steps, a bank of controls flickered with lights and dials. Beside it was an enormous vat brimming with custard that seemed to glow in the dark.

That wasn't the worst news.

Dangling above the gloop was a large net containing a dozen of their school friends.

Stan recognised a few of his class and wondered where the rest were being kept. It was clear that Dr Sinister was planning some ghastly experiment but there was no sign of him – maybe he was on a tea break.

Stan felt Minnie's hand on his arm.

'It could be a trap,' she whispered. 'Remember what it says in the *Pocket Guide*?' Stan shook his head; unfortunately, he hadn't read that far.

PROPERTY OF
MIGHTY HIGH SCHOOL

DON'T BE GOOD,

BE SUPER.

The Pocket Guide for Superheroes

Everything you need to know
to save the world.

DEADLY DEATH TRAPS

Death traps – don't you just hate them?
You would think that evil villains had
better things to do than dream up
ingenious ways of killing their enemies.
Sadly, this is how they get their kicks.
Deadly Death Traps come in many forms,
but here are a few you should avoid:

1. THE MOUSETRAP

2. THE DEADLY DELIVERY

3. THE SLIDING FLOOR

4. THE FIENDISH FALSE DOOR

If you do find yourself caught in a deadly death trap, try to keep calm and escape by using your superpowers. If you possess titanic strength or laser-beam eyes, you should be fine. If you're super-ticklish, you may be in a spot of trouble.

Finally remember the golden rule: if it looks like a trap and smells like a trap, it probably *is* a trap.

If Stan had read this good advice, he might not have marched forwards, setting off the alarm.

WOOP! WOOP! WOOP!

Suddenly a brick wall parted like a pair of curtains. Dr Sinister swivelled round, seated in his Director of Doom chair. Beside him stood the faithful Otto.

'Welcome to my humble laboratory,' said Dr Sinister. 'I must say I'm disappointed. I was hoping for more than a few super-halfwits.'

'We are **the Invincibles** and we're here to stop you,' said Minnie defiantly.

'How very original,' sneered Dr Sinister. 'We met before, didn't we? I should have guessed right away there was something wrong with your school. But in the end it's all worked out rather well. What better way to test my invention than on a bunch of super-brats?'

'You wouldn't,' said Stan.

'Oh, but I'm evil, so I would!' smirked Dr Sinister. 'Don't you remember your old friend?'

Tank emerged from the shadows. He seemed to have grown bigger and blobbier since the last time they'd seen him.

'Tank was lucky. He was the first to be transformed by Evil Custard,' said Dr Sinister. 'The effect of one bowl is impressive, don't you think? But what would happen if you dipped

some kiddies in a *whole vat* of custard, hmm?
Shall we find out?'

Dr Sinister pulled a lever. A cable ran out
and the net suddenly lurched towards the vat
of custard.

'AAAAARGHHHHHH!'

The prisoners inside swayed just above the ghastly gloop.

'STOP! Let them go!' cried Stan.

'Or else you'll tell your mummy?' sneered Dr Sinister.

'Or else this,' said Miles, pulling something from his pocket. Stan and Minnie followed his lead.

Dr Sinister had had enough of playing games. He pointed a finger.

'Obliterate them, Tank!' he ordered.

'Uhh?'

'GET THEM, YOU BRAINLESS BLOB!'

Tank obeyed and lumbered forward, hurling bolts of custard. One direct hit would be enough …

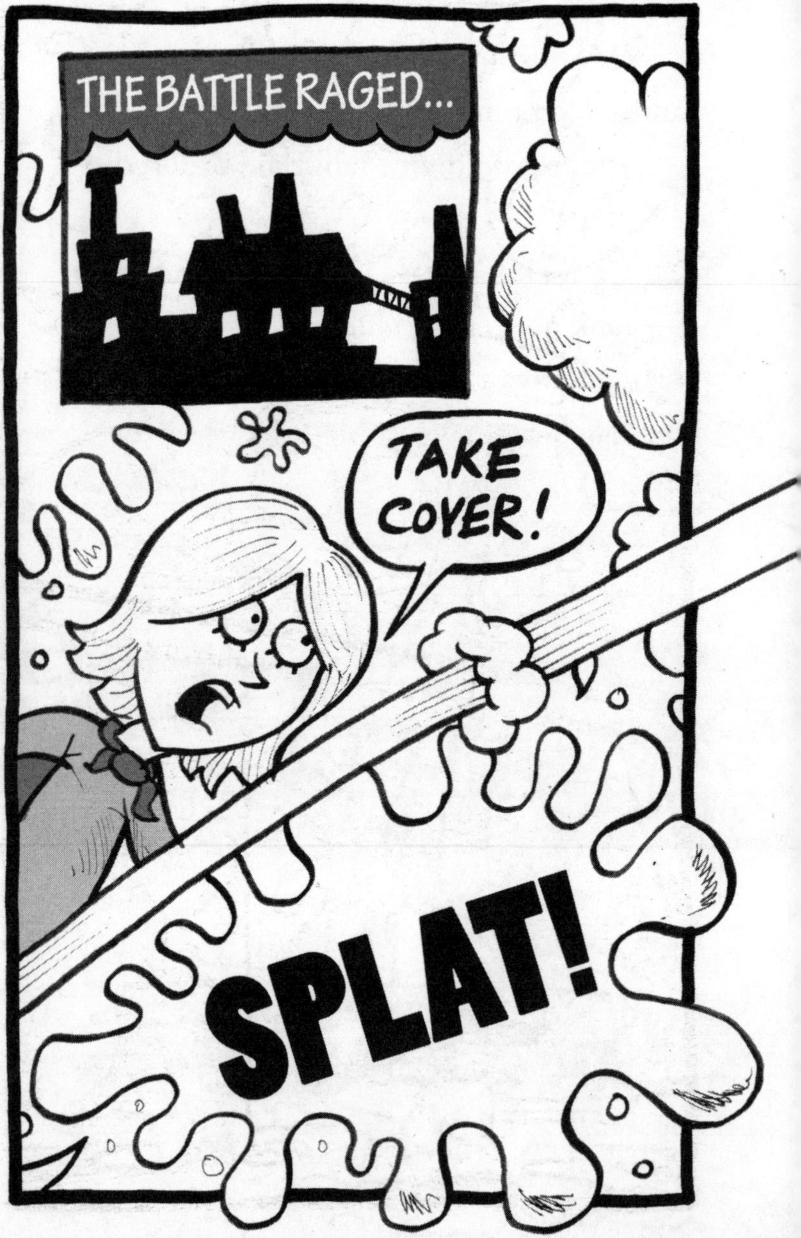
THE BATTLE RAGED...
TAKE COVER!
SPLAT!

Chapter 11

Bubble Trouble

Minnie squirted her frisbee clean and tucked it back in her belt.

'I think that went pretty well,' she said. 'Now to rescue the others.'

But they had forgotten Dr Sinister.

'You fools!' he cried. 'Evil Custard cannot be stopped!'

He yanked the lever and the net fell through the air, hitting the custard with a sickening splash. Ripples spread out across the pool and bubbles began to rise to the surface.

'That can't be good,' said Stan.

Out of the evil gloop rose a blobby head, followed by another and another – all with the faces of their school friends.

'DESTROY THEM!' shrieked Dr Sinister,
waving his tiny fists.

The Invincibles backed away.

'Um ... what do we do now?' asked Miles.

'There's only one thing we can do,' said Stan. 'RUN!'

They raced for the door as the first of the custardy creatures crawled dripping from the tank. Stan stumbled into the next room. Ahead he could see the door to the yard where Pudding was waiting. The Wonderdog barked and ran forward to meet them.

'Hurry up! They're coming!' panted Miles.

But Stan slowed down and stopped.

'What are you doing? *Come on!*' urged Miles.

Stan shook his head. 'All our friends are back there,' he said. 'We can't just run off and leave them!'

Minnie nodded. 'Stan's right. Dr Sinister has to be stopped before he makes an army of Evil Blob Things.'

'Like those, you mean?' Miles pointed a finger. They turned to see the giant Evil Blob Things advancing like ranks of yellow zombies. Stan raised his water pistol and took aim.

'Wait till they're close. On my signal,' he whispered.

'… NOW!'

Stan rolled his eyes. Terrific! They'd run out of water! This is it, then, he thought, curtain time. What a way to go, slimed by your own school friends with foul-smelling custard!

Pudding ran to hide behind Minnie, leaving a trail of wet paw prints. Wait a minute ... *wet paw prints?*

Stan looked up and for the first time he noticed the familiar drumming sound on the roof. Of course!

'OUTSIDE! QUICKLY!' he yelled.

They turned and raced outside. The Evil Blob Things wobbled slowly after them into the daylight. As the first raindrops fell on their heads, the creatures looked up and realised their mistake.

Soon there was nothing left of them but a dozen dazed children, sitting in puddles of runny gloop.

'Thank goodness for British weather,' said Miles. 'I was worried for a moment there.'

But there wasn't time to draw breath – there was still Dr Sinister to deal with. They found the potty scientist in his laboratory.

'Stop right there!' cried Stan.

'YOU!' gasped Dr Sinister. 'But that's not possible!'

Miles shook his head. 'You should know if you mix water and custard you get a runny mess. It's not rocket science.'

Dr Sinister ground his teeth. 'You will pay for this,' he snarled, reaching for the lever.

'Get him!' cried Stan.

Minnie took aim. The frisbee hummed through the air and struck the crazed genius on the side of the head.

Dr Sinister staggered back, losing his balance …

Chapter 12
School Report

Two days later the school inspectors stood in Miss Marbles' office, ready to deliver their final report. For some reason they had asked Stan and his friends to be present. Miss Marbles sat stiffly in her chair as if in the dentist's waiting room. Even Pudding stopped wagging his tail and rested his head on his paws.

'Well, I must say this week has been a new experience,' said Miss Miller. 'It's the first time I've spent a morning locked in a freezer.

Usually we are greeted with a cup of tea.'

Miss Marbles groaned quietly.

'In any case, our inspection is complete, so here is our report,' said Mr Long, placing a black file on Miss Marbles' desk. The head teacher took a deep breath and put on her reading glasses. The room fell silent. Stan could tell from the head's grim expression that it wasn't good news.

Inspection: Mighty High School

TEACHING – Awful. Key subjects are not taught well or even at all.

STAFF – Abysmal. One teacher could not spell 'Literacy'.

STANDARDS – Appalling. Books not marked, homework unheard of.

FACILITIES – Antique. Dismal classrooms, damp kitchens, dreadful food.

LEADERSHIP – Absent. The children are encouraged to make their own decisions!

Summary: C minus. By any normal standards of education Mighty High fails on every count.

Miss Marbles closed the file with a heavy sigh and pushed it away. Stan and Minnie exchanged worried looks. What now? If the school had failed the inspection, would Mighty High be closed down altogether, as Miss Marbles had feared? If that happened, they'd all be sent back to their old schools. **The Invincibles** would be broken up and they might never see each other again. Worst of all, none of them would get the chance to pass their final exams and become real superheroes.

Miss Miller picked up the file from the desk. 'However,' she said. 'It's clear to us that Mighty High is not an ordinary school teaching ordinary children. It could be argued that it should be judged by different standards. Take Stan and his friends, for instance ...' She turned to them. 'If it wasn't for you, Dr Sinister's plan might have succeeded, and who knows what else could have happened? Your courage and quick thinking are a credit to this school and your teachers.'

Stan didn't know what to say. His ears had turned pink, though for once it was nothing to do with danger.

'So taking this into account, we have decided not to submit our report,' said Miss Miller.

Stan watched in astonishment as she tore the pages into pieces and dropped them in the bin.

Miss Marbles stood up. 'But what will happen to the school?' she asked.

'Nothing at all,' replied Miss Miller. 'You can carry on training children to be whatever they want to be.'

'Superheroes,' answered Minnie.

Miss Miller smiled. 'I wouldn't know anything about that, of course,' she said, appearing to wink at them.

'Of course not,' said Miss Marbles. 'Well, I can't begin to thank you!'

And that seemed to be that. The inspectors shook everyone by the hand,

and walked out, leaving them in peace.

As soon as they'd gone, Miss Marbles sank back into her chair. 'Thank heavens!' she groaned. 'I'd rather eat Mrs Sponge's carrot trifle than go through that again.'

She settled her glasses on her nose. 'Well,' she said. 'It looks like once again I have you three to thank for saving the school.'

'Us four,' corrected Minnie. 'Pudding helped too.'

'Of course; my apologies, Pudding,' laughed Miss Marbles.

They turned to go, but Stan hung back. 'Just one last thing,' he said. 'What about Dr Sinister? Is he going to prison?'

Miss Marbles shook her head. 'That's the funny thing,' she said. 'Apparently if an evil person has too much Evil Custard, it produces the opposite effect.'

'You mean it makes him *less* evil?' said Miles.

'Exactly,' said Miss Marbles. 'In fact, he's

really quite sweet now. I'm told he's abandoned science and taken up a new job.'

LOOK OUT FOR MORE

SUPERHERO SCHOOL

ADVENTURES

LOOK OUT FOR MORE

SUPERHERO SCHOOL

ADVENTURES